PUSS
IN BOOTS

A free translation
from the French
of Charles Perrault

PUSS

IN BOOTS

WITH PICTURES BY
Marcia Brown

CHARLES SCRIBNER'S SONS, NEW YORK

PRINTED IN THE UNITED STATES OF AMERICA

15 17 19 21 23 25 27 29 RD/C 30 28 26 24 22 20 18 16

ISBN 684-12988-4

PUSS IN BOOTS

Once upon a time there was a miller who died and left no more riches to his three sons than his mill, his ass and his cat.

There was no need for a lawyer to divide the property. The eldest son took the mill, the second the ass, and the youngest was left nothing but the cat.

The young fellow was wretched at having so small a share. "My brothers," said he, "can make a living well enough by joining fortunes. As for me, when I have eaten my cat and made me a muff of its skin, I shall die of hunger."

The cat pretended not to hear all this. He spoke up seriously, "Do not fret, master. Just get me a sack and have a pair of boots made for me so that I can run through the brambles. You'll see that you are not so badly off as you think." The cat's master did not put much stock in what he said. But he had seen how clever Puss was at catching rats and mice—hanging by his heels or hiding in the meal playing dead. So he did not altogether give up hope.

When the cat had what he wanted he pulled on his boots with a flourish. Tossing his sack about his neck, he took the strings in his two front paws and hied himself off to a warren where there were a great many rabbits. He put some bran and

sow-thistles into the sack. Then, stretching out as if he were dead, he waited for some young rabbit who had not yet learned the wiles of the world to poke his nose into the sack, looking for something good to eat.

Puss had scarcely settled down when his plan began to work. A giddy young rabbit nibbled his way into the sack. Quickly pulling the strings, the master cat caught and killed him at once.

Quite puffed up
with his prize, Puss
marched straight to the
palace.

"I wish to speak to the king,"
he told the guards.

They showed him into the royal apartments.
Bowing low before His Majesty, he said, "Here, Sire, is a
wild rabbit from the warren of my lord the Marquis of
Carabas." (That was the name Puss was pleased to give his
master.)

"Tell your master," said the king, "that I thank
him and that his gift gives me great pleasure."

Another time the cat hid in a wheat field, ready with his sack open. When two partridges stepped in unawares, he pulled the cords tight and caught them both.

Off he went to the palace to present them to the king, just as he had done with the rabbit.

The king received the partridges with even greater pleasure. "See that Puss is properly rewarded," he said.

For two or three months the cat caught wild game like this, each time taking it to the king as a gift from his master.

One day Puss learned that the king was planning to take the air by the river with his daughter, the most beautiful princess in the world. So he said to his master, "If you follow my advice, your fortune is made. All you have to do is bathe in the river in a spot I'll point out to you. Leave the rest to me."

"Well, I can't imagine what good will come of it, but I'll do what you say," said the young man, and he and Puss set off for the river.

Now while the young man was bathing, the king happened to pass by. As soon as the cat saw the royal carriage approaching, he began to shout with all his might. "Help! Help! My lord the Marquis of Carabas is drowning!"

At these cries the king stuck his head out of the carriage door. "Why, it is the cat that brought me the wild game! Run to the aid of the Marquis of Carabas!" he called to his guards.

While the guards were pulling the poor marquis out of the river, the cat strode over to the royal carriage.

"Oh, Sire, my master had just stepped
into the river to bathe when two
robbers stole out of the thicket and
made off with his clothes! I chased them,
yelling, 'Stop thief!' at the top of my lungs,
but they were too fast for me!"

(The sly rogue had hidden
the clothes himself
under a stone.)

"Quickly,
fetch one of my best
suits for the
Marquis,"
the king ordered
the officers of his
wardrobe.

Off they dashed to the palace
and returned with a handsome coat of rich
brocade, with breeches and hat to go with it. The
king made a great deal of the young man. He was
a tall and handsome young fellow, and since the beautiful
clothes showed off his good looks, the daughter of the
king found him very much to her liking. The Marquis
of Carabas had only cast two or three respectful and somewhat
tender glances in her direction when she fell madly in love with him.
The king would have nothing but that the marquis enter the carriage
and take the air along with them.

The cat, delighted at the way his scheme was working out, marched on ahead. He came to some peasants who were mowing a meadow and said, "My good people, tell the king when he passes by that the field you are mowing belongs to the Marquis of Carabas. If you do not, you will be chopped into mincemeat!"

When the carriage rolled by, the king noticed the fine field. "To whom does this land belong?" he asked the mowers.

"To my lord the Marquis of Carabas," they said all together, for the cat's threat made them tremble.

"You have a splendid estate," said the king to the marquis.

"As you see, Sire, this field yields a rich harvest every year."

The master cat, still keeping well ahead of the carriage, met some reapers. He said to them, "My good people, tell the king that all this wheat belongs to the Marquis of Carabas. If you do not, you will be chopped into mincemeat!"

A moment later the king passed by, and of course he
wanted to know, "To whom does this wheat belong?"

"To my lord the Marquis
of Carabas," called out
the reapers.

Again the king congratu-
lated the young man,

And the cat, still trotting ahead
of the carriage, gave the
same warning to everyone
he met.

At last Master Slyboots came to a great castle, owned by the richest ogre ever known, for all the lands through which the king had passed belonged to him. The cat had taken care to find out who this ogre was and just what he could do. He demanded to speak to him, telling the guards, "I did not wish to pass so close to the castle without having the honor of paying my respects to your master."

The ogre received the cat as politely as an ogre could and bade him sit down.

"They tell me," said the cat, "that you have the power to change into all sorts of animals, that you can, for example, turn into a lion or an elephant."

"True," said the ogre brusquely, "and to show you, I shall turn into a LION!"

Puss was so terrified at the sight of a lion in front of him that he scrambled up to the gutters. And this was not easy, for his boots were of no use for climbing on the slippery tiles. Soon, however, the ogre resumed his natural form, and Puss jumped down.

"Well now, you really gave me a scare," he said. "But I have also heard, though I can hardly believe it, that you can take the form of the tiniest animals, for example, a rat, or even a mouse. I swear, that must be impossible."

"Impossible!" roared the ogre. "You shall see!" Quick as a flash he turned into a mouse and scuttled over the floor. The cat had no sooner spied him than he pounced on him and ate him up.

Meanwhile the king came by. When he saw the magnificent castle of the ogre, he wished to step inside. Hearing the rumble of the carriage wheels on the drawbridge, the cat ran out and announced, "Your Majesty is welcome to the castle of my lord the Marquis of Carabas!"

"How, my dear Marquis!" cried the king, now thoroughly amazed, "this castle is also yours? I have seen nothing finer than these superb buildings around this courtyard! Please,

let us go inside." The marquis gave his hand to the young princess. Following the king, who went first, they entered a grand hall. There they found a magnificent feast, for the ogre had invited some friends of his, who now were afraid to come in, for the king was there. The king was completely won over by the simple charm and character of the Marquis of Carabas, as was his daughter. By now the princess loved the marquis to distraction.

After drinking five or six glasses of wine and seeing the vast estate about him, the king said, "If you wish to be my son-in-law, my dear Marquis, it rests entirely with you."

Bowing very low, the marquis accepted the honor the king
bestowed upon him.

That very day he married the princess.

Puss became a great lord. Never again
did he hunt a mouse, except for sport.